Tennis Trouble

BY JAKE MADDOX

illustrated by Tuesday Mourning

text by Chris Kreie

Librarian Reviewer
Marci Peschke
Librarian, Dallas Independent School District
MA Education Reading Specialist, Stephen F. Austin State University
Learning Resources Endorsement, Texas Women's University

Reading Consultant
Mary Evenson
Middle School Teacher, Edina Public Schools, MN
MA in Education, University of Minnesota

STONE ARCH BOOKS
www.stonearchbooks.com

Impact Books are published by Stone Arch Books
151 Good Counsel Drive, P.O. Box 669
Mankato, Minnesota 56002
www.stonearchbooks.com

Library of Congress Cataloging-in-Publication Data
Maddox, Jake.
    Tennis Trouble / by Jake Maddox; illustrated by Tuesday
Mourning.
    p. cm. — (Impact Books. A Jake Maddox Sports Story)
    ISBN 978-1-4342-0781-4 (library binding)
    ISBN 978-1-4342-0877-4 (pbk.)
  [1. Tennis—Fiction.] I. Mourning, Tuesday, ill. II. Title.
PZ7.M25643Te 2009
[Fic]—dc22   2008004299

Summary: Even though she's only in seventh grade, Alexis made the
varsity tennis team. But some other girls on the team aren't happy she's
there.

Art Director: Heather Kindseth
Graphic Designer: Kay Fraser

1 2 3 4 5 6 13 12 11 10 09 08

Printed in the United States of America

TABLE OF CONTENTS

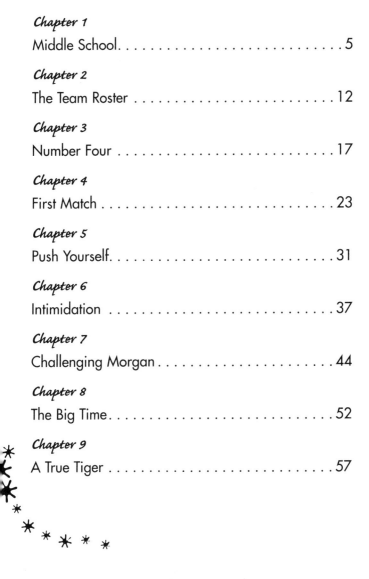

✳ CHAPTER 1

MIDDLE SCHOOL

Alexis Fletcher rolled the tennis ball around in her fingers. She bounced it three times on the court. Then she tossed the ball into the sky.

Whoosh!

Her arm came forward. Her wrist snapped like a whip.

Alexis hit the ball hard. It bounced inside the four straight lines of the service box, just across the net.

The ball quickly sailed past the arm of her opponent. Then it crashed loudly into the fence behind the court.

"Wow! Do that again," Coach Taylor shouted, walking next to the court.

Alexis tossed another ball up. *Whoosh!* Again, the ball landed in the service box before bouncing sharply to the left. The other player didn't have a chance.

As the coach watched, Alexis hit over several more serves. It seemed like her plan to impress Coach Taylor was working.

Coach Taylor was the head coach of the Fairfield Tigers. Today was tryout day for the Tigers high school tennis team.

Alexis was only in seventh grade. She'd thought long and hard about even coming to tryouts.

She had worried that trying out for the high school team while she was in middle school was a mistake. What if the older girls made her look bad?

After several more killer serves, Alexis looked around. Many of the other players were crowded around, watching her.

"Hey Coach. Mind if I step in?" Olivia Hamilton asked, walking over to Coach Taylor. Alexis knew that Olivia was the best player on the team.

"Sure, Olivia," said Coach Taylor. "Go ahead."

The tall senior girl trotted onto the court. "Let me see what you've got," Olivia shouted at Alexis.

Alexis took a deep breath. Olivia seemed really tough.

Alexis served the ball toward Olivia, who pulled her racquet back, preparing for a forehand shot.

Olivia made one quick step to her right. She smashed the ball back across the net.

Alexis jerked to her left, but it was too late. She missed.

"Hey, Middle School," shouted Morgan Gunderson, another senior girl. "No more tricks up your sleeve now that you've got some real competition, huh?"

Alexis tried to ignore her new nickname. She took a deep breath and got ready for another serve.

"Same as before, Olivia," Morgan shouted.

Smash! Alexis served the ball high above her head.

Olivia took a giant step to her right, but the ball whizzed by her racquet and into the fence. The other players hooted and hollered.

"Okay, players," shouted Coach Taylor. "Bring it in."

Alexis heard Morgan say, "You'll get her next time, Olivia." She patted Olivia on the back and narrowed her eyes at Alexis.

"Good job today, all of you," said Coach Taylor. "I think this season is going to be great." She looked at each girl before continuing. "You all should be proud of yourselves," she said. "I hate to cut anyone, but I have to. So, check the locker room door tomorrow morning for the list of players who made the team. If you didn't make it this year, I hope to see you back next year."

The girls jogged off the court. Another player ran up alongside Alexis. "Hi. You're Alexis, right? I'm Erin. You were amazing out there today."

"Thanks," said Alexis.

"No, really, you were great," Erin said. "Everyone said they'd never seen anything like it."

Alexis was shocked, and proud. "Really?" she asked shyly.

Erin nodded. "You're going to make varsity for sure, and you're only in seventh grade!" she said. "That's wild. I'll be happy just to make the ninth-grade team. But varsity? Wow."

"We'll see," said Alexis, smiling.

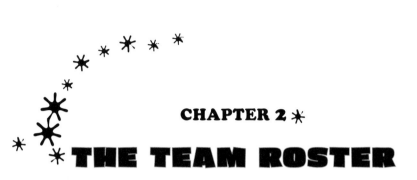

CHAPTER 2 ✳

THE TEAM ROSTER

The next day before school, Alexis's mom dropped her off at the high school. She couldn't wait to check the team roster. As she walked toward the locker room, she saw a group of girls gathered outside.

Erin stepped out of the crowd and ran up to Alexis. "Way to go! I told you you'd make varsity!" she said.

Alexis hardly believed her. "Are you sure?" she asked.

Erin nodded, smiling. Alexis let out a deep breath. Her dream to play varsity tennis was coming true!

"What about you?" she asked Erin.

Erin smiled widely. "I made the junior varsity team!" she said.

Just then, Olivia and Morgan walked up. "Step aside, girls," said Morgan. She waited for a few seconds for the crowd to part. Then she and Olivia walked up to the locker room door.

Olivia and Morgan looked at the team list. When they turned around, neither of them looked happy.

"Middle School!" said Morgan, looking out at the crowd. "You've got to be kidding me! Middle School made varsity? Has Coach lost her mind?"

Then she walked over to Alexis and said, "So, I bet you think you're pretty hot stuff, making varsity when you're what, ten?"

"I'm 13," said Alexis.

"Well, good for you," said Morgan. "You know what you did yesterday? You knocked one of my friends off the team."

"I'm really sorry," Alexis said quietly. "I didn't mean to." She saw Olivia comforting a girl who had tears in her eyes.

Morgan shook her head. "Oh, you didn't mean to?" she said angrily. "Well, it doesn't matter. Thanks to you, Rachel will be playing junior varsity. This is her senior year. This was her last chance. And because of you, she'll never play varsity."

Alexis felt awful. She didn't know what to do or say next.

"Are you just going to stand there?" asked Morgan. She stepped even closer to Alexis. Alexis saw Morgan clench her fists.

Olivia raced over. "Come on, Mo," she said. "It's not worth it." She pulled Morgan away. "Let's go."

Erin looked at Alexis and said, "Wow, nice way to start the season."

Olivia looked Alexis in the eyes. Then she shook her head and followed Morgan through the locker room door.

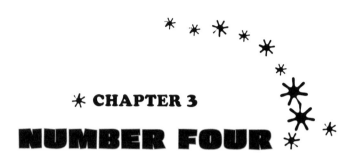

✳ CHAPTER 3
NUMBER FOUR

Before practice that afternoon, Alexis and Erin warmed up together.

"You're really good, Erin!" shouted Alexis across the net. She hit a backhand shot, reaching across her body to the left to hit the ball.

"Thanks," said Erin. "I'm better at doubles, though. Then I get to spend a lot of time hitting volleys up at the net. Go ahead. Hit me some."

Erin went closer to the net. She returned Alexis's shots, smacking each one back with a crisp, sharp volley.

Alexis was impressed. "Nice," she said.

"So, are you still worried about Morgan?" Erin asked, continuing to return Alexis's shots.

"Kind of," Alexis replied. "She seemed really mad earlier."

"Forget about her," Erin said. "She's just a loudmouth."

"But is it true?" Alexis asked slowly. "Did I knock Rachel off the team?"

"Well, sort of," Erin admitted. "But it's not your fault. Coach wants the best players to play on varsity, and you're one of the best."

Alexis hit a ball hard along the sideline. Erin couldn't even touch it with her racquet.

"Nice shot," yelled Erin.

"What about Olivia?" asked Alexis. "She seems okay."

"She's nice. I don't know why she's friends with Morgan, though," Erin said. She shook her head.

"She didn't seem too happy with me being on the team either," said Alexis.

"Olivia, Morgan, and Rachel planned on being on varsity together this year. Now they aren't," Erin said, shrugging.

"Okay, girls. Bring it in!" yelled Coach. The players gathered around the coach. She said, "Welcome to the first practice of the Fairfield Tigers tennis team!"

The girls all clapped. Coach Taylor said, "Congratulations to all of you for making the team. I'm not going to waste any time. I'm going to give you your positions right away, and then let you challenge each other to move up to higher spots during the season."

Alexis knew what that meant. Each girl would be ranked in order of talent. If someone wanted to get a better rank, she'd have to play for it.

After calling out the varsity doubles teams, Coach Taylor read off the varsity singles positions. "At number four will be Alexis, number three will be Stephanie, number two is Morgan, and number one is Olivia," she finished, smiling. "Congratulations, Olivia. You've earned it. Now make us proud this year."

"Thanks, Coach," said Olivia. "I will."

"Now, about the challenges," said Coach. "You can make two per week. And you can only challenge the player directly above you in the ranks. You play a one-set match. If the girl with the lower position wins, she moves to the higher position. Simple. Got it?"

All of the players nodded.

"All right then, let's practice," Coach Taylor said. "Twenty laps around the courts!"

Alexis couldn't stop smiling. Number four during her first year on varsity, and as a seventh grader? It was a dream come true.

✳ CHAPTER 4

FIRST MATCH

Two weeks after the Tigers' first practice, Alexis looked across the net at her opponent. She was playing against a girl from Oak High in the first match of the season.

The first player to win two sets would win the match. Alexis had lost the first set of the match. But in the second set, Alexis had come back to beat her opponent six games to four. Then the match was tied.

So far in the third set, Alexis had won four games to her opponent's five. She was close to losing the match. Her opponent only needed to win one more game to win the match.

Alexis wished she was serving, but it was the other player's turn to serve. The player who served always had more control over the outcome of the game. Alexis didn't like to give up that control, especially when she needed to win this game.

Alexis was ahead. But her opponent came back with two sharp serves. The game was tied.

Alexis was pumped to receive the next serve. She bounced on the balls of her feet and waited. The ball flew across the net and curved directly at her.

In a flash, Alexis took two giant steps backward and hit a shot across the net. It landed at her opponent's feet. The girl couldn't hit the ball back.

The score was 30–40. Alexis was one point away from winning the game and tying the set at five games to five.

Alexis got into position to receive the next serve. The ball was up high. Alexis's eyes got big. She tried to end the game with one shot. But she hit the ball too hard, too flat, and into the net.

Alexis planned to keep the ball in play on the next two points. If she could hit good shots, she could wait for her opponent to make a mistake.

She never had the chance. First, Alexis accidentally hit the ball into the net.

On the next point, her opponent hit a serve so hard that Alexis didn't even touch it with her racquet. It was an ace.

Just like that, the match was over.

Alexis jogged up to the net. She shook hands with her opponent. Then she left the court.

"Good job," said Erin, who was waiting on the sidelines. "You almost did it."

"Yeah," said Alexis. "But I didn't even win a game in the first set. I was so nervous."

"That's okay," Erin said. "These girls are tough. Only one girl on varsity has won so far. Junior varsity didn't win one match."

"Who's still playing?" Alexis asked.

"Olivia," said Erin. "Let's go watch."

Olivia was in the middle of a tough match. She was playing against the other team's number one singles player.

"That girl was on the doubles team that won the state championship last year," said Erin as she and Alexis neared the court. "She must have switched over to singles this year."

"Let's go, Olivia!" yelled Morgan from the sidelines. "Show her what you've got!"

"Morgan lost too," said Erin.

Olivia was amazing to watch. She moved quickly on the court, hitting back nearly everything her opponent could send to her.

"Man, Olivia is good," said Alexis.

"Tell me about it," said Erin. "But you're as good as she is."

"No way," Alexis said.

"You are. I can't wait to see the two of you play," Erin replied. "When you challenge her for the number one spot."

Alexis glared at Erin. "Dream on," she said. "I don't plan on challenging Olivia."

Olivia served the ball. When it came sailing back, Olivia smacked it deep into the court. She moved to the net.

Her opponent went for a lob, trying to hit the ball over Olivia's head. The ball sailed toward Olivia.

Olivia leaped up. She extended her arm for a backhand smash.

It was an extremely tricky shot. To do it right, Olivia had to turn her back to the net, jump as high as she could, and hit the ball above her head and backward.

She did it easily. The ball slammed into the far court and away from her opponent. Olivia had won.

Erin looked at Alexis. "You and Olivia. It's going to be a good match," she said.

CHAPTER 5

PUSH YOURSELF

A few weeks later, Rachel challenged Alexis for the last varsity singles spot for the third time. And for the third time, Alexis beat her.

After the match, Alexis went to the end court to grab some water.

"Beat her again?" asked Erin from behind the fence.

"Yeah," Alexis said.

"Well, don't act so excited!" Erin said, smiling.

"I kind of feel bad for her," Alexis admitted. "You know, since she's a senior and everything. I'd probably hate me too if I was in her shoes."

"She doesn't hate you," said Erin. "Besides, you're better than she is. That's clear. What are you going to do, let her win?"

Just then, Coach Taylor yelled, "Alexis! Come over here!"

"Uh oh," said Erin, laughing. "You're in trouble."

Alexis jogged over to the bleachers and sat down next to her coach.

"How are things going?" asked Coach Taylor. "Are you enjoying yourself?"

"Yeah," said Alexis. "I love playing tennis. And it's really cool to be on varsity."

"Good," Coach Taylor said. "You're a very talented player."

"Thanks," Alexis said.

The coach looked out at the courts. "So, Alexis. When do you plan to challenge Stephanie for the number three spot?" she asked.

"I'm not sure," Alexis replied. "I'm happy being number four. I think that's a good spot for me."

"But Alexis, you and I both know you're better than that," Coach Taylor said. Her voice was serious. She went on, "The only reason I put you at number four was because I wanted to see you earn a higher ranking. But now I'm a little disappointed."

"Oh," Alexis said. She felt awful. "I'm sorry, Coach."

Coach Taylor relaxed a little. "Don't be sorry. Just push yourself. I want to see you push yourself, and you aren't."

"But I'm only in seventh grade!" Alexis said. "I'm happy just being on the team."

"That's not good enough for me, Alexis," Coach Taylor told her. "I want to see you be your best."

"But Coach, the older players can't stand me already. If I start challenging them, they'll really hate me," Alexis said.

Coach Taylor shook her head. "That's their problem, not yours," she said. "Did you know that Morgan beat two seniors her sophomore year to earn the number three spot?"

"No," Alexis admitted. "I had no idea."

"She's been there. So have the other girls," Coach Taylor said. She smiled at Alexis. "Just tell me you'll think about it."

"Okay," Alexis said finally. "I'll challenge Stephanie."

✳ CHAPTER 6

INTIMIDATION

At practice the next week, Alexis and Erin hit ground strokes back and forth across the net.

"Nice match with Stephanie the other day," said Erin. "You creamed her. I'm so glad you decided to start making some challenges for a higher rank. Now everyone will really be able to see what you can do."

Alexis ran down a ball in the corner and hit it back to Erin.

"It's not a big deal," said Alexis. "I really just want to play tennis."

"Are you sure about that?" Erin asked, smiling. "You're challenging Morgan today for the number two spot, aren't you? Something tells me you want to do a little more than just play tennis."

"Be quiet and hit the ball, would you?" Alexis said with a laugh.

Erin hit a shot that pushed Alexis behind the baseline, which marked the end of the court. Alexis stepped back and hit the ball.

Erin hit another shot, and another. Each time, she pushed Alexis further and further behind the baseline.

"You don't have to hit it that well!" said Alexis, out of breath.

Then Erin stepped into the ball and hit it hard. She moved her racquet quickly under the ball. The ball barely cleared the net. Finally, it landed several steps in front of Alexis.

Alexis didn't have a chance. She almost fell over as she tried to get to the net. The ball bounced a couple of times before it finally stopped.

A voice came from the next court. "You need to move up on those, you know." Alexis looked up. It was Olivia.

"Those big shots deep in the court that drive you behind the baseline," Olivia went on. "You need to move up on those. Don't get so far behind the baseline. That's the problem you're having.

"Yeah?" Alexis replied nervously.

"Let me show you," Olivia said. She ran over to Erin's side of the net. "May I?" she asked.

"Sure," said Erin.

"Go ahead," Olivia told Alexis. "Hit me some deep shots."

Alexis hit a huge shot. It flew deep into Olivia's court.

Then Olivia stepped up. She barely waited for the ball to drop. Then she immediately smacked it back across the net and past Alexis's racquet.

"You can't wait for the ball to bounce so high," said Olivia. "You need to get the ball right after it bounces. Otherwise, your opponent will drive you too far behind the baseline."

"Okay," Alexis said. "Thanks."

"So, you're taking on Morgan today?" Olivia asked.

"Yeah," Alexis replied.

Olivia smiled and said, "Just remember, Morgan's going to try to intimidate you. Don't let her."

"Why are you telling me this?" Alexis asked, feeling confused. "You want me to win?"

"No," Olivia said. "I just don't want to see you lose to someone intimidating you. Tigers don't lose that way."

"Hey, Middle School!" yelled Morgan from the next court. "Let's play."

"Besides," Olivia added, "even if you beat Morgan, you're never going to get past me for the top spot." She winked at Alexis.

Alexis smiled. "Right," she said. "Well, I have to go beat Morgan now."

Then Alexis jogged to the next court, where Morgan was waiting.

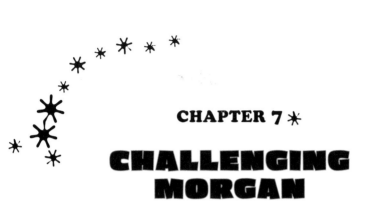

CHAPTER 7 *

CHALLENGING MORGAN

After playing for nearly an hour, Alexis was ahead of Morgan five games to four. Just one more game, and she would win the set.

Because this was a challenge match, not an actual match, Alexis only needed to win this one set to win the match. They didn't play best two out of three sets like they did in matches with other schools. That would make it easier for her to win.

Alexis felt very confident, mostly because it was her turn to serve. Morgan had struggled against her serve all match.

Alexis opened with a hard serve. Morgan hit a forehand back. "Try to get that one, Middle School!" she yelled.

Alexis hit a shot deep into Morgan's court. Then she moved to the net.

Morgan stepped forward. She got ready to hit the ball.

"Here it comes," Morgan yelled. She smacked the ball and delivered a winner into the far corner.

The score was Love–15. Morgan had won the first point.

Alexis tried not to get too nervous. It was only one point. Nothing to worry about. She could still win.

Following her next serve, Alexis quickly ran to the net. She wanted to shorten the distance. Hopefully, that would help her get to Morgan's next shot before it even had a chance to bounce. Just the way Olivia had told her.

Morgan drilled the ball right at Alexis. The shot was easy. Alexis pounced on it and hit it for a winner. The score was tied at 15–15.

Alexis looked around. Most of the players on the other courts had stopped playing. They were all watching her play against Morgan.

Morgan won the next point by getting to the net really quickly and slamming a shot that went far out of Alexis's reach. The score was 15–30.

On the next point, Alexis didn't waste any time. She hit a serve hard, right at Morgan's body.

Morgan barely got out of the way of the ball, but couldn't manage to hit it over the net. The score was tied, 30–30.

Two more points, thought Alexis. *Just put two more good points together and the match will be over.*

Alexis lined up her serve and took a deep breath. She hit the ball high above her head. Morgan waited and sent the ball back toward Alexis.

Alexis tried to stay calm. *Hit good shots*, she thought. *Don't go for too much. Take it easy.*

She hit a soft shot back to Morgan. Then she went to the net.

Morgan tried to hit a lob over Alexis's head, but it was not nearly high enough.

Alexis stepped back and went into a motion that looked a lot like her serve. She reached up high with her arm and slammed the ball across the net. It hit the ground several steps away from Morgan.

Alexis pumped her fist. "Yes!" she yelled happily.

Alexis looked at Erin. She and the girls around her were going nuts. The score was 40–30.

One more point, Alexis thought. *Just one more point.* She took a deep breath and got ready to serve.

Alexis served. Morgan returned it with a forehand that she smashed deep into Alexis's court.

Alexis played it on her back foot. Morgan hit another one deep. Alexis took another step backward and punched the ball across the net. Morgan grunted and hit another huge forehand.

Then Alexis remembered Olivia's advice: *Attack the ball. Don't let it attack you.*

Alexis lunged forward and hit the ball. As it flew to Morgan's side of the court, Alexis ran up toward the net.

Morgan reached out and hit the ball back with a weak backhand.

Alexis was waiting. She took a step forward and sent the ball away from Morgan. The match was over.

Erin ran onto the court. Alexis smiled as her friend hugged her. "Great job!" Erin said. "That was an awesome game."

Morgan slammed her tennis racquet into the ground. The racquet bounced up and smacked Morgan in the elbow.

Olivia walked onto the court and put her arm around Morgan. "Don't worry, Mo," she said. "You'll get her next time."

Olivia walked with Morgan off the court. But as she did, she turned around and gave Alexis a tiny smile.

CHAPTER 8 *

THE BIG TIME

Two weeks later, the Tigers' team bus pulled into the Roosevelt High parking lot.

"So, how many years has it been since we've won a match against the Mustangs?" asked Alexis.

"Eleven," Erin said. "In other words, practically our whole lives."

The bus squeaked to a stop. One by one, the girls piled off.

Alexis looked around at the freshly mowed grass and the neatly trimmed trees. The tennis courts were surrounded by flowers. The school was really nice. Alexis let out a deep breath. This was the big time.

"Well, if it isn't Motormouth Morgan Grundman," said a Mustangs player from inside the fence.

"Good to see you, too, Huffington," said Morgan. "Ready to lose and cry like a baby?"

"Oh, you mean like you did last year?" the player replied. The other Mustangs around her laughed.

Erin whispered to Alexis, "That's Mindy Huffington. Last year Morgan had six match points against her and still lost. It was pretty bad."

"Prepare to look silly this year," said Morgan. "We're going to be on you like stink on a monkey."

"Poor little Morgan," said Mindy. "She talks a good game. Too bad she can't back it up. How many times have I beaten you? Oh yeah, that's right, now I remember. Five."

Morgan laughed. "Whatever," she said.

"I hear there's a middle-schooler playing against me this year," said Mindy. "Are you really that scared of me?"

"Nah, just tired of you, that's all," Morgan said.

"Nice racquet, by the way," said Mindy. "I see you saved up for the expensive one from the drugstore." She turned and walked away.

Morgan stared into Alexis's eyes and said, "Middle School, you better beat her. You hear me?"

"I hear you," said Alexis.

"Good," Morgan said. "I'll see you after the match, when we celebrate our team win."

✳ CHAPTER 9

A TRUE TIGER

Alexis felt great.

Her backhand was working. Her forehand was working. She felt like she had enough energy to play ten sets.

Alexis had beaten Mindy Huffington easily in the first set, winning six games to two. And in the second set, Alexis was on track to win the match. She was ahead five games to one. She knew she would win the last game too.

It was Alexis's serve. She bounced the ball, tossed it, and then sent it across the net.

Mindy hit it back low, but Alexis was able to knock it back. She quickly moved up to the net.

Mindy hit a weak shot, which Alexis nailed for a point. Alexis was ahead. The score was 15–Love.

"Finish it off," someone said.

Alexis turned around. It was Morgan. Olivia was standing next to her.

"How did you guys do?" asked Alexis.

"We won," said Morgan. "Of course."

"So far, all of us have won," said Olivia. "If you beat Mindy, we'll win all of the matches."

Alexis nodded. Then she turned back to face Mindy.

Alexis served to Mindy's forehand. Mindy fired a deep ball back. Alexis attacked it and sent a shot deep to Mindy's backhand. Mindy hit it back.

Alexis hit the next shot to Mindy's forehand, forcing her to run to the opposite corner. Mindy barely got her racquet on the ball.

Then Alexis moved forward and swung at the ball in mid-air. She hit the ball deep into the court and away from Mindy. The score was 30–Love.

Alexis lined up her next serve. She decided to go for a big serve to Mindy's right that would take her out of position and leave most of the court open.

It worked. Mindy hit a weak shot back to Alexis. Alexis stepped into the shot and drilled it into the open court. The score was 40–Love. Alexis was winning.

"Go Alexis!" Erin yelled. Alexis looked behind her. Olivia and Morgan were still watching too.

Alexis took a deep breath. She bounced the ball three times.

Then she went for it. Her racquet flew through the air and struck the ball. In a flash, the ball cleared the net, landed in the service box, and bounced past Mindy's swinging racquet.

Mindy's racquet didn't even touch the ball. It was another one of Alexis's famous aces. It was also match point.

Alexis had won!

The players behind Alexis went nuts.

After shaking hands with Mindy, Alexis ran off the court. All of her teammates were there, cheering for her. The players all hugged her at once.

"Alexis," said Olivia, "that was awesome. You're a true Tiger."

Morgan stood behind the crowd. "You all done or what?" she said. The other players looked at Morgan and got quiet.

Morgan smiled and stepped toward Alexis. She held up her hand. Alexis slapped it as hard as she could.

Morgan nodded her head. "Not bad, Middle School," she said. "Not bad at all."

✳ ABOUT THE AUTHOR ✳

Chris Kreie grew up playing tennis on cracked blacktop courts that had chain-link fences for nets. It wasn't until his senior year that his high school started a tennis team. Chris joined the team and has been playing tennis ever since. Chris lives in Minnesota with his wife and two children. He works as a school librarian, and in his free time he writes books like this.

✳ ABOUT THE ILLUSTRATOR ✳

When Tuesday Mourning was a little girl, she knew she wanted to be an artist when she grew up. Now, she is an illustrator who lives in Knoxville, Tennessee. She especially loves illustrating books for kids and teenagers. When she isn't illustrating, Tuesday loves spending time with her husband, who is an actor, and their son, Atticus.

GLOSSARY

challenge (CHAL-uhnj)—to invite someone to try to beat you at something

competition (kom-puh-TISH-uhn)—a contest

confident (KON-fuh-duhnt)—having a strong belief in one's own abilities

disappointed (diss-uh-POINT-id)—let down because something hasn't happened as planned

expensive (ek-SPEN-siv)—costing a lot of money

intimidate (in-TIM-uh-date)—to frighten

opponent (uh-POH-nuhnt)—someone who is against you in a contest

position (puh-ZISH-uhn)—the place where someone is

rank (RANGK)—the position someone is in, in order of ability. The better your ability, the higher your rank.

varsity (VAR-sit-ee)—the best team at a school

TENNIS WORDS

Tennis, like most sports, has some words with special meanings. Here are some of the words used in tennis. These words were all used in this book.

ace (AYSS)—a point won with one hit

backhand (BAK-hand)—a stroke that starts on the opposite side of the body from the arm that holds the racquet

baseline (BAYSS-line)—the line at the back of the tennis court

doubles (DUB-uhlz)—a way of playing tennis with two people on each side of the net

forehand (FOR-hand)—a stroke that starts with the palm facing the way the stroke will move

game (GAYM)—one part of a tennis set

lob (LOB)—to hit a ball high into the air

Love (LUHV)—in tennis, a score of Love means zero points

YOU SHOULD KNOW

match (MACH)—the entire contest between two players

match point (MACH POYNT)—the point that wins the match

racquet (RAK-it)—the paddle used to hit balls in tennis

return (ri-TURN)—hitting the ball back to the other player

serve (SURV)—to send the ball to the other player to begin the set

service box (SURV-iss BOKS)—the area of a tennis court from which a serve is played

set (SET)—one part of a tennis match

sideline (SIDE-line)—the line on each side of a tennis court

volleys (VOL-eez)—an extended exchange of shots

Scoring note: In tennis, scoring isn't 0-1-2-3. Instead, it's Love-15-30-40! The next point after 40 wins.

DISCUSSION QUESTIONS

1. Why was Morgan mean to Alexis at the beginning of this book? What made her change at the end?

2. Alexis didn't want to challenge the older girls at first. Why not? What would you have done in her situation?

3. Should younger kids be allowed to try out for high school sports teams? Why or why not?

WRITING PROMPTS

1. Pretend that you're Alexis. Write a diary entry about your day at Roosevelt High, playing against Mindy Huffington.

2. Sometimes it can be interesting to think about a story from another person's point of view. Try rewriting chapter 8 from Morgan's point of view. What does she feel like during this chapter? What does she think? What does she see and hear?

3. Even though she was nervous, Alexis tried out for the varsity tennis team. Write about a time when you did something even though you were nervous.

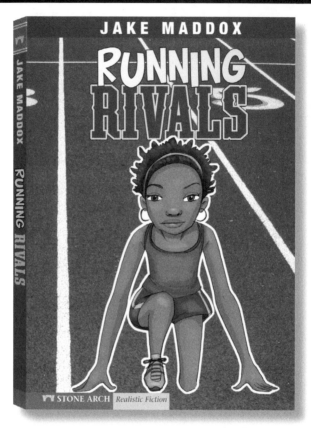

Amy hurt her knee during a race. Her knee healed, but her confidence is still broken. The biggest race of the year is coming up, and it's on the exact same track where she was hurt before. With help from an unexpected source, will she be able to race again?

BY JAKE MADDOX

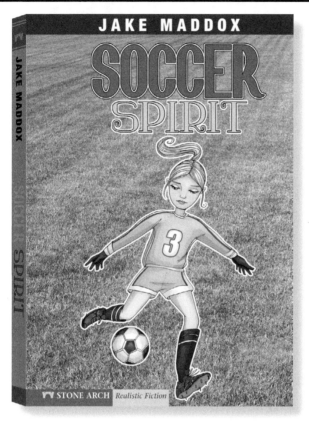

Anna, Brittany, and Jasmine have a problem.
Their school canceled the girls' soccer team.
They have to join the team at their arch rival
school! The players on their new team aren't
very nice. Will the girls ever feel at home?

INTERNET SITES

Do you want to know more about subjects related to this book? Or are you interested in learning about other topics? Then check out FactHound, a fun, easy way to find Internet sites.

Our investigative staff has already sniffed out great sites for you!

Here's how to use FactHound:

1. Visit *www.facthound.com*

2. Select your grade level.

3. To learn more about subjects related to this book, type in the book's ISBN number: **9781434207814**.

4. Click the **Fetch It** button.

FactHound will fetch the best Internet sites for you!